DATE DUE

SNOW COMPANY

SNOW COMPANY

BY Marc Harshman

ILLUSTRATED BY
Leslie W. Bowman

COBBLEHILL BOOKS/DUTTON · NEW YORK

All day long we've watched the snow falling and now here it is—a blizzard—and school's out early! I can't believe it! All the way home I watch the bus leave black tracks on the white road.

"Hey! That was close!" Ronnie's snowball hits the mailbox behind me. He gets me with the next one. "OK. You win," I say.

"But you didn't even fight."

"I know, but Mom's going to want us inside, and besides, I'm cold. Race you in!"

And it is cold, too. The wind and snow sting our faces. I know that Mom doesn't want Ronnie sick again. He's already missed too much school. Boy, don't I know. I hate having to carry his books plus my own.

Mom is mixing up corn bread for chili when we get inside. "Think there'll be school tomorrow, Mom?"

"There might be," she says between the flour and the milk, "but I don't know for sure."

"They could still have it?" She nods. "Oh, Mom, really?"

"I don't know, Teddy. Turn on the radio. I really haven't had a chance to listen yet."

Although it is still afternoon, it's almost dark outside. I've never seen anything like it. Mom tells us to get busy and help her clean the house. She says it's good for boys to learn to clean. Well, I'm not so sure, but I am sure I want the cocoa she promises for afterwards.

I can smell the cocoa everywhere by the time I'm done.
Outside I can see snowdrifts stretching across the field. One
starts at the mailbox and reaches almost across the road.

We drink the cocoa while Mom asks about school. Then
Ronnie takes a nap and I start the book Grandma got me for
Christmas. Mom calls me to help her in the kitchen a few
times, but I don't mind that, stirring bowls and measuring
cups and licking spoons. And outside the snow never stops. It
comes inch after inch, hour after hour. The radio says it's the
worst in twenty years.

Suddenly, in the middle of my book, I hear tires whining.
"Mom!" I yell, but she's already at the door, looking out into
the swirling snow.

"I can't see anything, can you, Teddy?"

But just then we both see the pickup, not on the road, but down in the ditch beside our crossroads. "It's Jim, Mom," but before I can even get my boots on, he's slammed his door and, with his lunch pail, is tramping through the drifts toward us.

"Heck of a storm," he says, smiling, "heck of a storm."

Mom asks if the mailbox drift did it, but no, he tells us, it's the wind blowing the snow so hard that he just couldn't see where he was. Then Mom tells him that our dad will be home soon. She tells Jim to make himself at home. He doesn't argue. Maybe he smells Mom's chili and corn bread—that would have been enough to make me want to stay.

Jim is drinking his second cup of coffee when I hear someone knock. I run to the door.

"Mrs. Hart?!" Boy, am I surprised. "Mom!" I shout and then to Mrs. Hart, "How are you?" I almost whisper I'm so surprised.

"I'm fine, Teddy. May I come in?"

"Yes, Ma'am." I hadn't even asked her in, that's how surprised I am. The old lady was plastered with the white dust of the snow except for where her face was red.

"Well, Ethel Hart, my goodness!" Mom is surprised, too, and even more when Mrs. Hart tells us to get outside to help Mrs. Mason and her baby. Her truck got stuck just after Mrs. Hart's car did.

Mom lets me go out with Jim. The snow just keeps coming and the wind blows harder. The crossroads are drifted shut. Even our mailbox is completely hidden except for the red metal flag sticking up through the top of the drift.

"I don't think your Mama's mail is gonna get far tomorrow," Jim laughs.

"You mean there won't be any school, either?"

"You can count on it, young Ted."

Mrs. Mason is still in her truck. Jim helps her wrap her baby in a blanket and a feed sack. She follows Jim back to the house and I follow her. It feels like marching, lifting one foot high, then the other.

It's almost dark when we get inside. Where's Dad? He should be home by now. I'm a little worried but I don't tell Mom. Just as we all sit down for supper, the phone rings.

"You get it, Ted." Mom smiles.

It's Dad! And he's fine, but he's stuck back in town.

"I'll stay with Grandma Price tonight. You and Mom and Ronald OK?"

Then I tell him all about our company. He thinks it sounds like a party, and he's right.

What a great night! The chili is great, the corn bread great, the company great. Mom would say "delicious," "crumbly," and "polite," but I like my way best. Ronnie thinks it's a great night, too. Ronnie, who drives me crazy with his riddles, has found that Mrs. Hart can not only guess his riddles, but has dozens of her own.

> What won't go up the chimney up,
> But will go up the chimney down?
> What won't go down the chimney up,
> But will go down the chimney down?

An umbrella! Even I admit that's pretty good. I like her, too. She was Dad's teacher at the old Wayne School. She acts like a real lady with her square shoulders and words like "grand" and "gracious." I love hearing her tell tales on Dad. A snake in Jenny Richmond's desk! My dad? I can't believe it.

Jim is great, too. He says he had walked over most of this country and tells us about copperhead swamps and squirrel trees and our Indiana banana. He says I might find it in a schoolbook under "pawpaw." Mrs. Hart nods her head.

Outside the snow is still falling. Jim repeats that it is one "heck of a storm." The wind never stops. The shed behind the house is buried under a perfect drift. But inside we're safe and warm.

Losing the electricity makes the evening even better. I help Mom gather every candle in the house. There are half-burnt Christmas ones, tall tapers, and fat ones in glass, reds and greens and whites, and even a purple one. We light the kerosene lamp for the table and sit there listening to story after story about everyone's past snows, like the big one of 1950.

Young Mrs. Mason helps the stories around, too. She tells us what her grandma and grandpa have told her. She tells how one winter her grandpap saved the pet duck by chopping it out of the horse trough with an old axe.

I could listen all night but everyone is getting sleepy. Jim curls up in a chair and Mrs. Hart sleeps on the sofa on the other side. Between them Mrs. Mason and her baby are put on the floor with sleeping bags and heavy comforters. Mom would offer our beds but she knows it's warmest by the stove.

The candles are blown out one by one and then I can hear the wind rattling the eaves and thundering on across the countryside. I wake up later. The wind has stopped and it's quieter than anything I've ever heard. When I look out the window, I can see that the snow is nearly finished. The moon is slipping in and out of the clouds.

I peek into the living room and see everyone sleeping under their blankets, under all the quiet. I'm happy to watch them. Jim is sleeping in his bibs. Pretty Mrs. Mason has her baby all curled in her arms, and Mrs. Hart, just like a lady, has her hands folded on her chest like a statue. I'm glad for it all—the snowy night, our house, the quiet, glad I'll have my own story the next time company comes.

For my parents—MH
For Doris—LWB

Library of Congress Cataloging-in-Publication Data
Harshman, Marc.
Snow company / Marc Harshman ; illustrated by Leslie W. Bowman.
p.   cm
Summary: Teddy and his family enjoy the excitement of unexpected company
when their neighborhood is hit by the worst blizzard in twenty years.
ISBN 0-525-65029-6
[1. Snow—Fiction.   2. Blizzards—Fiction.]
I. Bowman, Leslie W., ill.   II. Title.
PZ7.H256247Sn   1990
[E]—dc20   89-23941
CIP   AC

Published in the United States by
Cobblehill Books, an affiliate of Dutton Children's Books,
a division of Penguin Books USA Inc.

Typography by Kathleen Westray
Printed in Hong Kong   First Edition
10 9 8 7 6 5 4 3 2 1